Hailey Twitch

and the Great Teacher Switch

Hailey Twitch
and the Great Teacher Switch

Lauren Barnholdt
Pictures by Suzanne Beaky

sourcebooks
jabberwocky

Published by Sourcebooks Jabberwocky, an imprint of Sourcebooks, Inc.
P.O. Box 4410, Naperville, Illinois 60567-4410
(630) 961-3900
Fax: (630) 961-2168
www.jabberwockykids.com

Library of Congress Cataloging-in-Publication data is on file with the publisher.

Source of Production: Versa Press, East Peoria, Illinois, USA
Date of Production: January 2011
Run Number: 14440

Printed and bound in the United States of America.
VP 10 9 8 7 6 5 4 3 2

For Aaron, always

Contents

Chapter One

One New Friend

I have a very big secret. And that secret is that I have a magic sprite. Her name is Maybelle and she has long sparkly blond hair and beautiful glittery wings and she came flying out of my magic castle last week. She lived in there for two hundred whole years and I, Hailey Twitch, am the only one who can see her.

There are some good things about having a magic sprite, and some bad things. The good things are that no one else can see her. So it is like a big secret you have to keep to yourself! The bad things are that sometimes your sprite might get you into trouble for something that you did not even do. Like when Maybelle used a marker to draw on my skin and my teacher Miss Stephanie thought it was all my fault.

Also, Maybelle cannot even do any good magic. She got her magic taken away because she was not fun, like a sprite should be. But she is working on it. Which is why I am in the bathroom at school right now, even though we are right in the middle of having a Countries of the World Party in room four, Ms. Stephanie's second grade. I had to leave that very fun, fun, fun party because Mr. Tuttle is in the girls' bathroom.

Mr. Tuttle is the head of the Department of Magic. And he is here to make sure that Maybelle is getting fun. Otherwise she will not be able to get her magic back.

"Now," Mr. Tuttle says. "We have to talk about Maybelle. It is very important."

Mr. Tuttle is a little scary. He is just as tall as me with a very big belly. Also, he has big black glasses and a clipboard. A clipboard is where grown-ups write bad things about you. Like if you start being bad and need a good punishment. Unfortunately, I know all about that.

"I guess so," I say. I wonder if I can tell him to hurry up, please. I am missing the party where Antonio Fuerte is maybe going to do a special Mexican dance. Antonio Fuerte is one of my friends. He has black hair and black eyes, and today he is wearing a sombrero.

"Maybelle needs to work on having more fun," Mr. Tuttle says. He looks at me over his glasses. His eyes are very big under there. "And so you, Hailey, are going to be in charge of her."

"You mean…you mean like the boss of her?" I say. Suddenly, I am paying very good attention! This is very happy news, even better than being at the party! I love being the boss of people! And now I am the boss of my very own magic sprite! It is official.

"Yes," Mr. Tuttle says.

Maybelle just sits there on the sink. She is getting her new sparkly green dress all dirty on the bottom. And she looks very nervous. I give her a little pat on the back. But she does not seem too cheered up.

"Now, one of the things Maybelle must do in order to become more fun," Mr. Tuttle says, "is to make one new friend."

"One new friend?" I try not to seem like a snob about this. But making one new friend is very easy. I just made one new friend named Addie Jokobeck. "Are you sure that's all?"

"Yes," Mr. Tuttle replies. "And you will report back to me on how she is doing."

"Yes, sir!" I give Mr. Tuttle a salute just like they do in the army. "How should I report to

you?" I ask. "Should I maybe give Maybelle a report card?"

"No," Mr. Tuttle says.

"Should I give her a student of the month for friendship if she is good?"

"No," Mr. Tuttle says.

"How about if I—"

"Hailey!" Mr. Tuttle says. "Please. I will come back in one week, and you will tell me if Maybelle has made a new friend. That is all." And then there is a little blue flash like lightning, and Mr. Tuttle is gone. Well. I guess that means I will not be getting my very own clipboard. But oh well. I am still the boss of Maybelle!

"Oh, no!" Maybelle says from the edge of the sink.

"I do not think it is too clean in there," I tell her. "One time I saw Megan Miller have a big runny nose in that sink."

"How am I going to make a friend?" Maybelle asks. She looks like maybe she is going to cry any minute. "I cannot make a friend! I am doomed."

"You are not doomed," I say. "Don't worry. You can make a friend. I will help you." I give her my most best smile. "It will be very easy. And now it is time to get back to the party."

- -

There is not that much time left in the party. Just enough to see Antonio Fuerte do a special Mexican jig. And then it is time to go home. Maybelle is very quiet on the bus. I think she is thinking about making one new friend. But she does not have to worry for long!

And that is because when we are walk, walk,

walking home from the bus stop I see a big moving van across the street! It is big and white and it says GENTLE GIANT MOVERS on the side. I am very good at sounding out those words!

Moving vans mean one wonderful thing. And that is that new neighbors are moving in! New neighbors are very lucky if you can get them. Because they might have one girl your very own age. One girl who will play with you and maybe become your friend.

"I wonder who is moving into that house," I say to Maybelle. "I wonder if it is one very true friend my own age."

"Or one true friend for me!" Maybelle says. She starts to look happy. Her mouth goes twitch, twitch, twitching almost into a smile.

Then an old man sticks his head out from behind that moving van. He looks right at me. His eyes are very blue, like the sky. But his hair is very white and in two big puffs. Like big marshmallows with a bald spot in the middle.

"Hey, you," I say to him. But then I remember that is not what you say to new neighbors. I try to remember the important manners that I learned in first grade. "Excuse me," I try again. "Are you moving into that house, please?" I give him a smile. He might have one little girl that lives in there. One little girl that is his granddaughter and who will be my own true best friend! And maybe she might have shoes with roller skates on the bottom that she will let me borrow.

"Yes," he says.

"And do you have a granddaughter who is maybe my age who might live there with you?" I am at the bottom of his driveway now. And so I look up into his moving truck. He does not seem like he has anything too fun or funny in there. It is all brown furniture. No toys. Or games. And no pink princess bed.

"No, I do not," he says.

"Do you have a granddaughter that comes to visit you every weekend and likes to share her shoes?"

"No," he says. "I do not."

"Do you—" I start to say. But then I stop. Because the moving men are pulling something out of the moving van! And it is a gumball machine, the most amazing gumball machine I have ever seen. It is taller than me and has blue and white and red and green and orange and purple gumballs all in it! Maybe this is a good neighbor after all!

"Can I," I say very nicely, "maybe have one of those gumballs out of that machine if I have my own quarter?"

"No," the man says.

Wow. What a disaster of a neighbor. And

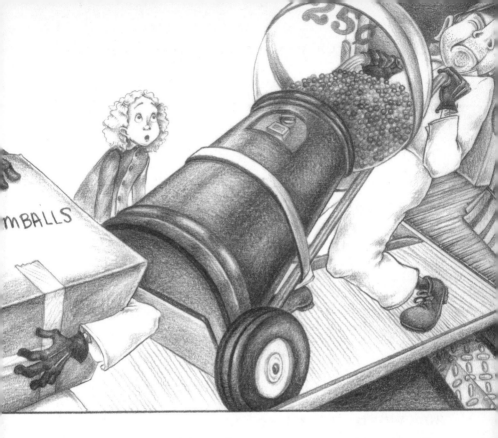

then that neighbor becomes even more of a disaster. He looks right at me and says, "And just so you know, I do not like kids."

And then he goes walking right into his house and slams the door behind him.

I think Maybelle is definitely maybe just a little bit crazy in her head. Because after that man said that mean thing about kids, Maybelle thinks he is going to be her friend.

"That man is going to be my new friend." Maybelle is zooming all around my head. "His name is Edgar Frisk. I read it on his mailbox!"

"Maybelle," I say, "I think you are a little bit crazy in your head. That man does not like children."

"I am not children," she says. "I am a magic sprite."

"Yes, but I am a child, and I am the boss of you. Mr. Tuttle even said." I am in the kitchen looking around for a good after-school snack. There is a new rule in my house. And that is that after-school snacks must be nutritious. I do not think I like that rule too much.

My mom comes into the kitchen "Hi, Hailey," she says. "How was school?"

She opens the refrigerator and pulls out an apple. And while the door is open, Maybelle sneaks in there and looks around.

"Nothing good in here," Maybelle says. "I am going to have Oreos! Oreos are fun because they are not healthy. And they are very messy." Then she flies right over to the cookie cupboard. Talk about rubbing it in.

"There is a new man across the street," I say to my mom. "He has very boring furniture except for one very humongous gumball machine, and he does not like children." I think my mom will be happy about this gossip. But she just looks worried.

"Oh, no," she says. "Hailey, what did you say to that poor man?"

"Nothing," I tell her. "Cross my heart. I just saw into

his moving van. And then he told me he does not like children."

"Hailey," my mom says. "You must make sure to stay away from our new neighbor, do you understand? He probably does not want to be bothered."

"Oh, I understand," I say. I do not want to be friends with that mean, mean, meanie anyway. I get a package of brown crackers with peanut butter. Then I sit down at the table.

And I do not know if it is my imagination playing tricks on me, but I think I hear Maybelle say, "But *I* will not stay away from him."

- -

Chapter Two

A Very Delicious Breakfast

The next morning Maybelle is waking me up very early. She is beating her wings very fast and brushing them against my nose.

"What time is it?" I ask. I push those soft sparkly wings away from me.

"It is six!" Maybelle is flying all around. She is making all the papers on my desk flutter in the air. "It is time to get up! It is time to spend the day making a new friend!" she says.

"Six?!" I say. "Are you crazy? Wake-up time is not until eight! That is when the little hand is on the eight and the big hand is on the twelve." Then I pull my covers over my head. "Go away."

"Please, Hailey," Maybelle says. She is down at the bottom of my bed. And she is pulling my covers right off me and down to the floor! "I have a very good plan about how we can get that man Edgar Frisk to be our friend."

"You are not going to be friends with that man," I say. "He does not like us. So forget it." I wiggle my toes back and forth. They are very cold with no covers.

"Not yet," Maybelle says. "But we can *get* him to like us." I think about this. She just might be right. Sometimes I have to grow on people.

"But how are we going to do that?" I ask.

"I think we should make Mr. Frisk a delicious breakfast." Maybelle flies down onto my pillow. "To be nice and make friends!"

I decide this is a very horrible plan. And that

is because my bed is warm. And also because if I am going to wake up early, it is so that I can watch cartoons.

"Maybe another time," I say. I sit up. "It is time to watch *Jungle Jingo* on TV before school."

Then Maybelle puts her hands on her hips. And she wags her finger right at me. And she says, "Hailey! Don't you want to help me make a friend?"

I think maybe not really. But I do not say this. I learned last year in first

grade that you should not always say everything that you are thinking in your head.

"We can do that tomorrow," I say. I give Maybelle a pat on the back so she will believe this lie. Usually it is not good to lie. I learned that rule all the way back in kindergarten. But this lie is to make Maybelle feel better. That is what's called a very important exception to a rule.

"HAILEY!" Maybelle yells. "DON'T YOU

WANT TO HELP ME GET MY MAGIC BACK SO WE CAN DO LOTS OF FUN THINGS WITH IT?"

"What do you mean?" I must admit I am a little bit interested in this. "Tell me all the fun things we can do with your magic if you get it back. Right now, please."

"We can do all the fun things that sprites do with their magic," Maybelle says. She does not sound so sure about it. Probably she does not know. I decide she needs a suggestion.

"Do you mean like getting me shoes with wheels on the bottom that turn into roller skates even though my mom said I am not allowed to have them?"

"Yes," Maybelle says. She is sitting on my pillow. And she is fluff, fluff, fluffing her hair.

"Well," I say. I jump out of bed. "When you put it that way, it is a very good idea to make that man some breakfast."

So me and Maybelle sneak downstairs. We are trying to stay quiet. If I am up too early my mom will say, "Hailey, why are you waking up the whole house?" No one else is awake yet. And they will not be waking up until six thirty. That is very lucky.

"Now let me see what we have for breakfast," I say to Maybelle when we are in the kitchen. I am opening cupboards all over the place. "We have cereal." I stop. "Stop right there," I say. "That is it! We do not have to go any further. I will bring Mr. Frisk some cereal!" Cereal is very easy to make. It is just cereal, milk, a bowl, and a spoon.

"I don't know," Maybelle says. "When I lived in the castle, we would always make a special breakfast for a special occasion."

"Cereal is special," I say. But I know deep down in my heart that it is not true. Cereal is not special. Cereal is the easy way out.

"Maybe we could make French toast!" Maybelle is very excited about this idea. She starts flying all around. Her wings brush against a picture on the wall, and it goes crooked.

"I do not know how to make French toast," I say. "But I do know how to make regular toast. Is that good enough?"

But Maybelle is having a one-track mind. Kind of like me when it comes to roller-skate shoes.

"French toast is just regular toast only with eggs," she says. "It's easy."

I open the refrigerator and take a good look. "We have lots of eggs!" I pull out a big carton. "And lots of bread!"

I jump up on the counter so I can get down one big bowl for those eggs. I am not *technically* supposed to be doing that on account of one time my big sister Kaitlyn did it when she was seven and she broke her arm. But this is a special occasion.

"Now Chef Hailey Michelle is going to break these eggs right into the bowl!" I announce. Michelle is my middle name. It goes very beautifully with Hailey. I look in the carton. One, two, three, four, five, six eggs left. That is very perfect. I think we are going to have to use all of them. This will be a big breakfast.

I crack those eggs and pour, pour, pour them into the bowl. Then I take out a whisker and whisk, whisk, whisk them right up. Then I put some salt and pepper in. Because that is what my mom does when she is cooking. I put in a lot just for good measure. A big cloud of pepper comes up and goes right in my nose!

"ACHOO!" I sneeze.

"ACHOO!" Maybelle sneezes, too.

"I want to help, I want to help!" she yells. "I am supposed to be friends with Mr. Frisk, and so I need to help, too!"

"Oh, yes," I say. "Good idea. You are Chef Hailey Michelle's assistant. You go and get the bread, cooking servant."

Maybelle tries to get the bread out of the bread box. But it is too heavy for her. She drops it on the ground. I am bringing the bowl of mixed-up eggs over to the toaster. And on the way I—oops!—step on that loaf of bread. It gets very squished.

"Oh, well," I tell Maybelle. "It is the thought that counts."

I tear open that bread sack. Then I shake that bread into the bowl of eggs. Then, when it is all good and ready, I put that bread right into the toaster.

"Now we have to wait until they pop up," I say.

"Okay," Maybelle says.

So we wait. For ten or more seconds. But it is taking too long, so finally, we just pop that French toast right up ourselves!

"Those look very soggy and wet," Maybelle says. She makes a bad face. She does not look like she likes that French toast too much.

"That is just because they do not have syrup on them," I tell her. I have a lot to teach that sprite. She does not even know about fun things like syrup. I grab the bottle of syrup and pour a big blob on top of some French toast. And then I have another wonderful idea. And it is because of something I remember! And that is that big beautiful gumball machine that Mr. Frisk was bringing in!

"Maybelle," I say. "In case you were

wondering, Mr. Frisk is very into candy." But Maybelle does not get it. I sigh. "So that means that we need to put more syrup on this plate immediately." I turn that bottle right over and squeeze, squeeze, squeeze the syrup right out.

"That seems like too much," Maybelle says. "You do not know about fun things like syrup," I tell her. "Syrup is just fancy brown sugar. I learned all about it one time on a field trip to a syrup factory."

I give the bottle one more good squeeze. Then I load everything all up on a plate.

"And now," I say. "We will bring this to Edgar Frisk!"

We creep out the door. And march across the street. I keep the plate very steady in my hands. I do not shake. I do not stumble. I do not trip, and I do not come even close to dropping that plate. And then, finally, I am there! On Mr. Frisk's porch! With a delicious plate of French toast in my hands!

I ring the doorbell. *Ding-dong.* But no one comes. I ring it again three times. *Ding-dong, ding-dong, ding-dong.* But Mr. Frisk is still not coming.

"We might have to do this plan later," I tell Maybelle.

"NO," Maybelle says. And then she swoops into the house through one open front window!

"Maybelle!" I shout. "Maybelle, come

back!" But Maybelle does not come back. She has gone inside Edgar Frisk's house! She is probably doing something very, very bad in there! Then I look on the bright side. And the bright side is that Mr. Frisk will not be able to see or hear her even. But still! She needs to get out of there right this instant!

"MAYBELLE! WHAT ARE YOU DOING? THAT IS AGAINST THE LAW!" I am really shouting loud. Like a crazy person even. Then I remember it is morning. People are asleep in their beds. And so I decide to tone it down. "Maybelle," I say a little softer. "You better get back out here right now!"

The neighbor next door is coming out to go to work. And she is looking at me like I am nutso. "Oh, hello!" I give her a big wave. "Nothing to see here. I am just visiting my new friend, Edgar Frisk!"

I think maybe that lady neighbor is going to

come over and see if anything is wrong. But then Mr. Frisk's door opens.

And Mr. Frisk is standing there! He is  wearing a pair of brown slippers. And a long red robe. And he looks…not so happy. Maybelle comes swoop, swoop, swooping out behind him.

"Hailey, I woke Mr. Frisk up by brushing my wings against his face, and then he did a big sneeze, and I do not think he is a morning person," Maybelle says. She bites her lip. She is looking very, very worried.

"If I give him this sugary breakfast it will

cheer him up," I whisper. "Do not worry. I am very good at making friends."

"Who," Mr. Frisk says, looking down at me, "ARE YOU?"

That is a very mean thing to say. But I will not be mean back. That is not how you make friends. "I am Hailey Twitch," I say. "And I am very pleased to meet you."

"It is SIX O'CLOCK IN THE MORNING!" Mr. Frisk yells.

"Yes, well, it is a very nice day out!" I say. This is not very true. It is kind of cloudy. And cold. And I forgot to wear my sweater.

"Give him the breakfast," Maybelle says. "Please, please, give him the breakfast!"

"Here is your breakfast," I say happily to Mr. Frisk. "It is French toast." I bend over and present it to him. Like I saw a waiter at a fancy place do once when I was out with my Grandma Twitch.

"French toast?!" Mr. Frisk frowns at the plate. There is a very big wet dripping mess on it.

"It has extra syrup," I tell him. "So don't be confused if it looks wet. It is just very *sugary*." I smile. "Would you like to eat it outside? Me and you could sit on these rocking chairs."

"That," Mr. Frisk says, "is some bread with raw egg on it." His face wrinkles up like it is very gross to him. "You are giving me a plate with some raw egg on it!"

"No," I say. "I am not. That bread went right into the toaster." This is really turning out to be a bit harder than I thought. "Also, you should know that I am very good at French cooking. One time me and my friend Addie Jokobeck made a whole big batch of French fries for our French cooking project." Mr. Frisk should be very proud of this fact. French cooking is not easy. But Mr. Frisk still looks very mad.

"MR. FRISK, YOU NEED TO HAVE SOME FUN AND EAT THIS FRENCH TOAST!" Maybelle screams. She is flying up by his ear and yelling right at him. Even though he cannot hear her. Then she picks a piece of that French toast right up. And she puts it up to Mr. Frisk's lips. And egg and syrup get all over him!

"Ahhh!" Mr. Frisk yells.

"Oh, I am so sorry!" I say. I am looking around for a napkin. That is the one thing I forgot! But I cannot be expected to think of everything.

"I am having fun, fun, fun," Maybelle says, flying all around.

31

"Like when you had that food fight with Addie Jokobeck."

"It is not nice to throw food at people," Mr. Frisk says. Then his big bushy eyebrows scrunch up real close together. "Please," he says. "Little girl, go home." And then he closes the front door right in my face.

Chapter Three

Mr. Spaghetti and the Second Grade Play

"I am very, very mad at you," I tell Maybelle on the way home. "You are not supposed to start food fights with grown-ups. You are not supposed to start food fights with anybody!"

"But he did not want to eat it," Maybelle says. "And so I was showing him how."

"He did not want to eat it because we did not make it right," I tell her. I do not know how or why, but I think something went terribly wrong with that French toast. "And now he thinks that I am the one that put that food in his face!"

I decide that I am going to have a tantrum very soon. I can feel it building up inside

me, just ready to come burst, burst, bursting out.

And when I get inside my house, it is about to come bursting out even more. Because my mom is waiting for me. And she says, "Hailey Michelle Twitch, what is this mess?" I look around. At the drip, drip, dripping eggshells. And the squish, squish, squished-in loaf of bread. And the stick, stick, sticky syrup that is all on the counter and the floor.

"This mess," I say. "Hmmm. Well, if you really want to know the truth, it has to do with a delicious breakfast."

"Ha!" Maybelle says. "Mr. Frisk did not think it was so delicious!"

"What kind of breakfast?" my mom asks. She is looking at the toaster. The toaster does not really look so good. It has egg dripping down all over it. Maybe it might even be broken.

"A breakfast of delicious French toast!" I say. Then I hold the plate out that I am holding. But now it is empty. Because I accidentally dropped the rest of the breakfast on Mr. Frisk's front porch.

Then my sister Kaitlyn comes into the kitchen. "What happened in here?" she asks. "What a disaster area." Kaitlyn is fourteen and she thinks she is very smart.

"Your room is a disaster area, Kaitlyn," I say. "And you are not the boss of me." I am really getting about to have a tantrum! And right before I have to go to school, too.

"Uh-oh," Maybelle says. She is looking out the window. "Mr. Frisk is coming to your door! Mr. Frisk is coming to your door! Quick, Hailey, run and hide!"

But it is too late. The doorbell rings very quickly three times. *Ding-dong, ding-dong, ding-dong.* This is turning into a very huge disaster of a morning.

"I am very sorry," I say to my mom. "But I am not feeling so well. I think I need to get back to bed, please." I put my hand to my forehead. "Feel my head," I say. "It is very hot from a fever."

"You are going to stay right there, Hailey," my mom says. She puts down the sponge she is holding and goes to the front door.

I tiptoe into the living room so I can hear. My mom and Mr. Frisk are talking in soft, soft, soft voices.

"Hailey?" my mom says. "Come here, please!"

"Yes?" I say. I put a look on my face. And that looks says this is all one big mistake.

"Did you bring Mr. Frisk some bread dipped in raw egg?" my mom asks.

"Mr. Frisk," I say to him, "now you know that is not true. I put that bread in the toaster. I even told you that!"

"Lying is not nice," Maybelle says, shaking her finger at him.

"Please," Mr. Frisk says. "Stay away from me and stay out of my yard." He is still wearing his red robe. And his dumb brown slippers.

"Hailey," my mom says. "Please go to your

room and get dressed for school. Then come and see me before it is time for the bus."

- -

My mom tells me that I will be grounded for one hour when I get home from school. I am not going to be allowed to watch anything fun on TV. Or call my friend Addie Jokobeck on the phone. Or play with Kaitlyn's old dolls when she is not looking.

I am very mad at Maybelle for getting me into this mess. But I cannot even tell her. Because after I get my punishment, she disappears and does not come back!

So by the

time the bus drops me off at school, I am in a very cranky mood. I put my coat away in my cubby. I sit down at my desk. And then I remember something won, won, wonderful! And that is that today we are going to be talking about the second grade play! The second grade play is put on by room four and room five. I have already decided that if it is the last thing I do, I will be in that play. Also, it would be very perfect if it could be this one very good play I know called *The Gingerbread Princess*.

"Good morning, Addie," I say to Addie Jokobeck.

Addie Jokobeck sits next to me in room four. The important thing to know about Addie Jokobeck is that she is really in love with rules. Also, her hair is always very smooth, smooth, smooth.

"Did you know that today we are going to be talking about the second grade play?" I ask.

"Yes," she says. Addie Jokobeck looks nervous about it.

But I do not have time to even ask her why. And that is because it turns out that there is a substitute in room four! A substitute is what you get when your teacher is out being very sick or having a baby or needing a break from a bad class. Some substitutes are very nice. They let you talk loud. They let you draw on the chalkboard. And sometimes they will let you play Heads Up, 7UP instead of doing work.

But some substitutes are very mean. They make you do lots of work. They make you stay very quiet. And they think they are big bosses even though it is not even their class.

"Good morning," our substitute says. He is a boy. I have never had a boy substitute before! This boy substitute might be enough to cheer me right up. That is because boys are easy to boss. Like my friend Russ Robertson. One time when we had a lemonade stand and made eleven whole dollars, I got to keep six of it, and Russ got to keep only five.

"Miss Stephanie is out with chicken pox, so I am going to be your substitute, Mr. Spametti."

"Excuse me, Mr. Spaghetti," I say, waving my hand high, high, high in the air. I stand up and smooth down the very beautiful blue

skirt I am wearing. "I just need to let you know that today we are supposed to be talking about the second grade play." I smile my very brightest smile and wait for him to pick me as the gingerbread princess.

"Yes, well, I don't know about all that," Mr. Spaghetti says. He gives a little laugh. He is sounding the same way my dad sounds when he is about to say no to something. "We'll see."

I look at Addie Jokobeck. Addie Jokobeck looks at me. I know we are thinking the same thing. And that is that when a grown-up says "we'll see" that means no, no, no.

I get a dark look on my face. But then Maybelle pops right up before I can even say anything.

"How can I make this fun, please?" she asks, zooming all around my head. Maybelle is wearing a very wonderful sparkly belt that I made her out of one of Kaitlyn's special hair ties. Kaitlyn left that hair tie in the bathroom. So that means finders, keepers.

"Nothing right now," I whisper very softly so that Addie Jokobeck cannot hear. "And I am still very, very mad at you. So you just sit and stay quiet."

Mr. Spaghetti is taking attendance. "Bailey Twitch?" he says.

"My name," I say, "is Hailey. You must be getting your *b*'s confused with your *h*'s."

"Oh," Mr. Spaghetti says. "Sorry about that."

"That is okay," I say. "Getting our letters confused happens to the best of us. Now will we talk about the play? Maybe Ms. Rancone could help us do it." Mr. Spaghetti looks confused. I sigh. This substitute is not too with it. "She is the teacher of room five," I explain.

"Ms. Rancone is out having a baby," Natalie Brice, the meanest girl in room four, says. Without even raising her hand! Natalie Brice thinks she is the boss of everything.

"The play," Mr. Spaghetti says, "will be on hold until Miss Stephanie gets back." And that is the end of that.

Chapter Four

- - - - - - - - - - - - - - - - -

A Disaster of an Apology

When I get home my mom is on the computer in the kitchen. She is laugh, laugh, laughing at something on the screen.

"Did you know," I ask her, "that the second grade play is canceled and Miss Stephanie has the chicken pox and we have a substitute whose name is Mr. Spaghetti?"

"Mr. Spa-metti," my mom says.

"How do you know?" I ask.

"Because I got a phone call from the school yesterday," she says.

"You knew all about this and you did not

even tell me?" I plop myself down real hard in a chair. "Keeping secrets is not nice," I whisper.

"Look at me, Hailey!" Maybelle says. I jump. She is just now popping up again after being gone almost all of the day. "What do you think of these new shoes? They are called high heels." She pulls up her dress and shows me these very gorgeous silver sparkly shoes. But I am not in the mood. On account of being grounded for one hour.

My mom is laughing again.

"What are you laughing at, please?" I ask. "Don't you know things are a disaster right now?"

"That man who moved in next door," my mom says. "Edgar Frisk, the one who you made very angry this morning. He was a famous actor when he was younger. I'm watching some of an old commercial he used to be on."

I run, run, run over to the computer. I look right at that screen. A man is taking a big bite of a piece of chocolaty cake. He is getting brown frosting all over his lips! "Mmm," he says.

My mom thinks it is fun, fun, funny. She is laughing her head right off.

"I do not think that is the same guy," I say. "Because that man across the street is not fun or funny." I want to say he is very mean. But I don't. That is because I do not want to be grounded for longer than one hour.

"Do you think my new friend Mr. Frisk is going

to like these shoes?" Maybelle asks. She is doing a little tap dance on the kitchen table.

"He is not your new friend," I whisper. "He is very mean."

"He is mad because I put egg on his face," Maybelle says. "But I am going to win him back."

"What?" my mom asks.

"Oh, nothing," I say. "Never mind." My mom gives me a weird look. I look back at the computer. Edgar Frisk is making everyone just laugh, laugh, laugh. They think he is really great at acting in that commercial. They are probably all going to run out and buy that chocolaty chocolate cake.

And then, suddenly, I am coming up with a plan. It just pops right into my head. That Mr. Frisk neighbor is an actor. And we need someone to help us do the second grade play. So all I have to do is get to be friends with Mr. Frisk and then he can help me save the play!

And then everyone at school will be so happy that they'll let me be the gingerbread princess!

"I am a genius!" I say.

"Why?" Maybelle asks.

"Why?" my mom asks at the exact same time.

I think about telling my mom my very genius plan. But then I remember something important. Something that I know about parents. If you tell them a very genius plan sometimes they do not think it is so genius. Sometimes they tell you that you cannot do that plan. Especially if a person who's a part of that plan called you "little girl" and said to please leave him alone. So I decide maybe to keep it a secret for now.

"Oh, no reason," I say, hoping she does not ask.

"Well," my mom says. She clicks out of Mr. Frisk's commercial. "Don't forget you are grounded, Hailey. I'm sorry that had to happen, because it was nice of you to think about making Mr. Frisk breakfast. But you know you shouldn't be in the kitchen cooking. Not to mention bothering that poor man." I quickly cross my fingers and say a wish that she will not ask me not to bother Mr. Frisk ever again. And my wish is answered! Because she doesn't. She just looks at the clock and says, "You will be grounded until four o'clock."

- -

I spend my hour of being grounded thinking about my plan. Also, I read one very good book. When that hour is over, my mom goes to the store. And she leaves Kaitlyn in charge of me. Kaitlyn is outside doing her homework on the front steps. And so right as soon as my mom is gone, I go outside to ask Kaitlyn for help.

Kaitlyn thinks she is very smart because she

is, actually, very smart. And sometimes she will let me wear her sparkly butterfly clips. But right now the reason I am interested in her is not because of her hair clips. It is because she is very good at coming up with ideas.

"Hello, Kaitlyn," I say when I see her.

"Hi, Hails," she says.

I love it when Kaitlyn calls me Hails! It is a new thing. I hope it catches on.

"Kaitlyn," I say. "What would you do if you made someone very mad?" I plop myself down in the grass and get ready to listen to one of her smart ideas.

"Why?" she asks. She is looking up from

the homework she is doing. And her eyes are very suspicious. "Did you take my apple shampoo again?"

"No," I say, shaking my head no, no, no. I hope she does not ask me if I took her special sparkly hair ties. I do not think she would like the answer to that.

"I think I accidentally used that shampoo," Maybelle says. She flies down in front of me. I take a big sniff of her hair. It smells like yummy crisp apples. Yikes.

"If I made someone mad," Kaitlyn says, "I would apologize. And then I would do something nice for them. Like maybe throw them a party."

"A party?" I wonder what kind of party Mr. Frisk would like. Maybe it is going to be his birthday soon! Maybe he is going to be turning one hundred! I do not think I could find a cake big enough to hold one hundred whole candles.

"Yes, like a surprise party at their house. Maybe with *boys*. But you cannot do that since you are only seven." Then Kaitlyn gives me a look. "But," she says, "you can apologize."

"Apologize?" Maybelle asks. "That is not very fun at all."

Then Maybelle gets a look on her face. I have seen that look before. It is the same look she gave me one time right before she started a food fight in Addie Jokobeck's kitchen. And then she poofs right away before I can ask her what she is up to.

I sigh. I guess I will have to figure this out all by my own self. I decide to sit down on the steps and think, think, think. I sit there for a very long time. I sit there so long that Kaitlyn finishes her homework.

And then she says, "Hails, I am going in the house to use the phone. Do NOT leave this yard." She makes me cross my heart and promise.

As soon as Kaitlyn goes inside, Maybelle comes back! And she is looking exactly like a very huge mess. Her sparkly yellow hair is covered in white dust.

"Maybelle," I say, "you are a very big mess." I am cough, cough, coughing at all that dust.

"Hailey!" Maybelle says. "I have come up with a very fun and wonderful idea! I have saved the day!" She stands on the porch. And does a twirl. And a bunch of white dust falls on the steps around her.

"What do you mean?" I want to know. I do not like this one little bit. I like to be the one that comes up with very fun and wonderful ideas. And I like to be the one who saves the day. Plus, I am the boss of Maybelle. Mr. Tuttle said so.

"I have given Mr. Frisk a perfect apology and surprise!" Maybelle flies into the air and does a loop.

"Oh, no," I say. I am getting a very bad feeling in my stomach. "Maybelle, what did you do? Tell me right this instant!"

"Look!" She grabs my hand and pulls me across the street. "Look, look, look!" She points down to the ground. I look. It is Mr.

Frisk's driveway. Maybelle has written all over it in chalk. The words are "I am very sorry, Edgar Frisk!" in big huge white letters.

"I do not know about this," I say. "We are always supposed to get a special permission to draw with chalk on the driveway. My dad even says."

"Yes, but this is an apology! An apology party in the driveway!" Maybelle flies all around my head, chalk dust flying out of her hair. "And it is fun." That sprite looks very proud of herself.

"Where did you get this chalk?" I ask.

Maybelle looks a little nervous for once. "I found it," she says.

"Maybelle Sinclair! That is a big fat lie and you know it!" I shake, shake, shake my finger at her.

"Fine," she says. "I took it from down the street in Jessie Brody's garage."

"Oh." I think about the time I had a bake

sale using store-bought cookies and Jessie Brody told everyone. I decide not to yell at Maybelle too much for being a thief. "But, Maybelle," I say. "You cannot just go around writing on people's driveways." Even I know that.

"But look at how beautiful this driveway is," Maybelle says. I look around. That driveway is very perfect for chalk writing. It is very long. And very smooth. I peek down at that bucket of chalk. It is a very humongous bucket with nice big fat sticks of chalk in a whole rainbow of colors. And suddenly my fingers are itch, itch, itching. They really want to reach out and grab that beautiful purple chalk and get to work!

"Well," I say, thinking about it. "Now that you already wrote 'I'm sorry, Edgar Frisk' then maybe I should just write my name so that he knows who is giving him that apology." I get down onto the driveway. I write my name. *Hailey*. Then I decide to write my last name, too, just in case. *Twitch.* That chalk feels wonderful sliding over the driveway! I have never felt such a smooth driveway! It is like writing on air!

I draw one little piece of candy near my name. That is because I think Mr. Frisk will like it. He has a gumball machine, after all. Then I write my new nickname "Hails" underneath it.

"I should stop now," I say to Maybelle. "Maybe after I draw a nice piece of cake on this driveway for Mr. Frisk." I draw one tiny piece of cake. And then I put that chalk down.

But my fingers are itch, itch, itching to pick it back up. And then, all of a sudden, it is like I have lost control! I cannot help it! I am drawing chocolates and peppermints and cupcakes and ice-cream sundaes and brownies with frosting and doughnuts with sprinkles and gummy worms and lollipops and candy canes and all sorts of things! Once I get started, I cannot stop! I am a drawing machine! Maybelle is helping, too. She is drawing pictures of magic sprites and candy castles.

It is very fun, fun, fun. Also, I am a very good artist if I do say so myself.

"We should get Kaitlyn to take a picture of this with her special camera," I tell Maybelle. "So that we can remember all our hard work."

"Good idea," Maybelle says. "We can show it to Mr. Tuttle so that he knows I am being fun, fun, fun!"

"You are getting pretty good at fun, I must admit," I say to Maybelle. But I do not realize that the fun is about to be over. And that is because all of a sudden, the door to Mr. Frisk's house flies right open.

"Oh, hello, Mr. Frisk," I say. I try to quick stand on the extra drawings me and Maybelle did. "Look at what I wrote to you!" I point to where it says, "I am sorry, Edgar Frisk." It is a little bit hard to see now. On account of one cupcake picture that is blocking it.

Mr. Frisk's bushy white eyebrows go all the way up, up, up on his forehead. I have never seen eyebrows fly up so far.

"*What*," he says, "have you *done* to the driveway?"

"Nothing," I say. "I just wrote on it. With

chalk only. Chalk comes right out." Mr. Frisk does not say anything. I think maybe he has never played with chalk before. Probably he is too old. So I say, "With water. It will come right out with water. Do you want to try? You could draw whatever you want!" I hold the piece of orange chalk out to him. I am very good at sharing. But Mr. Frisk does not take that chalk. He just stares.

"You," he says, "are a mess."

I look down at my pink T-shirt and my new jeans with the sparkly flowers on the legs. They are covered with lots and lots and lots of chalk dust. I do not think my mom will be too happy about that.

61

I decide that it is time to change the subject. "I heard," I say, leaning in close to him, "that you are a very famous actor."

"Who said that?" Mr. Frisk bends down and picks up that big bucket of chalk. He is reading the back of it. I wonder if he knows that he should give it back to Jessie Brody when he is done.

"I saw a commercial of you," I say. "On the computer. And now I would like to do some business with you, please."

"You want to do some business with me?" He is looking at me like I am the craziest person ever in the whole world.

"I have a job for you," I say. I cross my fingers behind my back so that Mr. Frisk will say yes.

"A job for me?" Edgar Frisk says. "You are only a little child!"

"Yes, well, I want you to help me with my school play!" I say. Edgar Frisk is looking very angry. So I decide to give it one last shot. "Also," I tell him, "you might even get my allowance if you want. Also, I am not very good at taking no for an answer." I cross my fingers again and hope he is going to say yes. But my dreams do not come true. Because Mr. Frisk does not say yes. He does not say no. He does not say anything. He just points across the street at my house.

So I turn around to walk back. And that is when my mom starts pulling into our driveway. And that is when Mr. Frisk walks quickly across the street and tells her everything about the chalk and the driveway and the very huge mess.

Chapter Five

The School-Yard Bully

My punishment is that I have to clean up Mr. Frisk's whole driveway. The whole, whole, whole, whole entire driveway! With all those beautiful and wonderful pictures on it. They are going to be washed right down the drain with a hose! That is called destroying art. And if that is not bad enough, then I have to help Mr. Frisk do some yard work. That is not fun or funny, not even one little bit.

I am so sad the next morning at school that I do not even get cheered up when Antonio Fuerte wants to play chase with me on the playground.

"Antonio," I say. "I am too very sad to play chase."

"Cheer up, cheer up, cheer up," he says. He is bouncing all around. "I have GOOD NEWS!!" Antonio Fuerte is putting his hands around his mouth when he says that so that it echoes all over the place.

"What is the good news?" I ask. I must admit I am a tiny little bit interested.

"The good news," Natalie Brice says, coming up and butting right in, "is that my mom is going to be the one who helps us with the second grade play."

I gasp. Mrs. Brice cannot be the one to do the play! Mrs. Brice does not like me for lots of reasons, including something having to do with Natalie's birthday party that was not even my fault.

"That," Maybelle says, "would be horrible."

"That is nice of you, Natalie," I say. "But that's okay. You can tell your mom never mind. Because that would not be fair."

"My mom would be very fair," Natalie says. Then Natalie does a little smile. And that smile means that if her mom Mrs. Brice comes to help us with the play, Natalie will get to be the star. Being the star of the play is the very best role! That is because people will say you are beautiful and you will get to wear the best costume and after it is over you will get to take a bow all by your own self on the stage. Plus, maybe you will even get some flowers.

"Yes, but maybe some other people's mothers want to be in on this play," I say. I bounce right over to my friend Russ Robertson. "How about you, Russ? Does your mom want to get in on this or what?"

Russ shakes his head. "I don't think so," he says. "My mom has to watch my brothers." Russ has two baby brothers named Carter and Jackson. They are very beautiful babies. But they are not allowed to be left alone.

"How about you, Addie? Wouldn't your dad like to be in on this play?" Addie's dad Mr. Jokobeck is very fun and funny. He would be very good at running the play.

"No, my dad cannot do it," Addie says. "He has to work." She is jumping rope. And her hair is not even moving. I reach up and feel my own hair. It feels like a big disaster area. Also, I think some chalk might still be in there.

"Maybe your mom can do it, Hailey," Addie says. "Or your dad."

But my mom and dad have to work, too. I wonder if they can take a vacation. A vacation to save the play! But then I remember they do not have any vacation. They are saving it all up for when we go visit my Grandma Twitch.

"Well, my mom does not have a job, and she does not have any little babies, so she can spend lots of time with us." Natalie Brice does a big smile and then she kick, kick, kicks her legs back up into a handstand. Doing handstands in the school yard is not allowed! But Mr. Spametti does not know that. I am itch, itch, itching to tell him. But I am not a tattletale, even though

Natalie Brice is the meanest girl in room four.

"And," Antonio says, "I am going to play the part of the bully." I am very confused by this. There is no part of the bully in the play of *The Gingerbread Princess*. *The Gingerbread Princess* is about a beautiful princess who lives in a gingerbread house. Also, she becomes friends with gingerbread children and saves them from an evil witch.

"There is no bully in *The Gingerbread Princess*," I tell Antonio. "I think you might be getting a little confused in your head."

"The play we are doing is called *The School-Yard Bully*," Natalie says.

"*Or* we might be doing this one very good

play I know about called *The Gingerbread Princess*," I say. I smile at Antonio and try to get him on board. "You can be the gingerbread prince," I tell him. I do not think there is a gingerbread prince in the play. But maybe we will write that part in later.

"We are doing the bully play," Antonio says. "Get away, bullies!"

"Antonio," I say. "Why are you telling the bully to go away when you are the bully?"

"Oh," he says. "I don't know." I give a big sigh. Antonio is really trying my patience. He should know that this news does not make me happy.

"We are doing *The School-Yard Bully*," Natalie says. "And that is that."

I want to tell her that maybe she needs to learn a lesson her own self about being a school-yard bully. But instead I just say, "Well, in case you are wondering, I have a big secret about another person who might be coming in to help us with the play."

"Who?" Antonio asks.

"Yeah, Hailey, who?" Addie Jokobeck asks.

"Yeah, who?" Maybelle asks.

"It is a surprise," I say. "A special surprise about a famous man that is coming here to help us save the play!"

"Yeah, right," Natalie says. "I really do not think so. You have no one to come in and do the play. And it does not matter anyway, because my mother is coming in this afternoon to help us."

"Well, that guy will be here tomorrow," I say. I cannot help it. Also, when you think about it very hard, it is not even a lie. Because I just need to convince Mr. Frisk! And I am very good at convincing.

"Tomorrow is Saturday," Natalie says. "So that is impossible."

"Well, he will be here on Monday," I say.

"And we will just have to see about what happens, because I highly doubt that we will be doing the play of *The School-Yard Bully*."

"The Schoollll-Yarrrdd Bullyyyyy," Antonio Fuerte yells. And then it is time for the day to start. So we all go inside. But I cannot stop thinking about Edgar Frisk. And how I can come up with a very smart, big plan to get him to help me.

Chapter Six

- -

Not the Way to Stick Out

After lunch is when we are all brought down to the auditorium to talk about the play! The auditorium is one of the very best places in the whole school. That is because it has a very big stage and a microphone. And lots of folding-down chairs to sit in. And spotlights. And an American flag on the wall.

"What is this place?" Maybelle asks.

"This is the auditorium," I say. "And if you do not behave in here, I am going to give you a bad report to Mr. Tuttle."

This makes Maybelle very nervous. And so she stays real quiet.

I sit down in a folding-down seat right next to Addie Jokobeck. She is holding her cup of teeth. Addie Jokobeck keeps all her baby teeth in a little tiny silver cup. Then she holds that cup when she is nervous. This is kind of a little bit strange. But Addie is my friend. So I try not to judge. Judging is when you think you are the boss of what another person is thinking or feeling. Kind of like when Natalie Brice called me one big baby last year just because I did not do so well at Megan Miller's sleepover and had to go home in the middle of the night.

Mr. Spaghetti is at the front of the auditorium on the stage. He does not look like he knows what he is doing.

"I am nervous," Addie says. "I do not like being up on the stage."

"It is okay," I say. "You will be fine." I give her a pat on her hand.

"Thank you, Hailey," Addie says.

Then someone pulls my hair from behind. It is Antonio Fuerte!

"Hola!" Antonio says. *Hola* means hello in Spanish.

"Hola!" I say back. "Antonio, you are loco!" *Loco* means crazy. I love learning Spanish words. It is a very smart thing to do.

"No, Hailey," Antonio says. "You are loca! You are loca because you said you had a big secret person to come in for the play and that is not true." Then I feel myself starting to get mad, mad, mad. But Antonio's eyes are black, black, black, and they are very sparkly when he smiles. So I have a hard time keeping up with my anger.

"It *is* true," I say.

"Then why didn't you bring him today?" Antonio asks.

"Because the person I am bringing got very sick today." Being sick is a very good excuse. "And that person is throwing up their breakfast all over the place. So he could not come today. But he will be here first thing on Monday morning!"

"That is a lie," Natalie Brice says. She is sitting in front of me, and she has been listening in on our conversation!

"Natalie," I say, sighing. "Spying on people is not very nice."

"It does not even matter about your secret person," she says. "Because we are getting ready to do the play of *The School-Yard Bully*!"

"Put up your dukes!" Antonio says. And then he puts up his dukes.

Addie Jokobeck clutches her cup of teeth.

Mr. Spaghetti starts to talk into the microphone. "Everyone in room four, please listen," he says. "Today we are going to be talking about the second grade play. We are being joined by room five." I look over to the other side of the auditorium. Room five is sitting there. I do not like room five because they have a guinea pig named Edward. Which is not really fair to room four when you think about it.

"Now, everyone, please welcome Mrs. Brice. She will be helping us do our play," Mr. Spaghetti says.

Everyone in the audience starts to clap, clap, clap! And then, before I know it, Mrs. Brice is coming out onto the stage! There is nothing I can do to stop it, not even one little thing!

"Hello, children," she says right into the microphone. She is dressed very fancy in a yellow lacy dress and yellow shoes that are high, high, high. She does not really look too much like a mom to me. Moms are supposed to wear jeans. And big sweaters. And T-shirts. And maybe some track pants for when they go grocery shopping.

Maybelle is sitting on my lap. So I lean down, down, down so I can whisper right in her ear. "I do not like Mrs. Brice," I say. "She is taking over the play."

"Oh, no!" Maybelle says. "And then Mr. Frisk won't be able to take over the play!"

"Yes, and then you will not be able to be his friend." I try to sound very innocent about all this. I do not want to be putting any ideas into Maybelle's head. About how she can maybe make things real hard for Mrs. Brice. But I also kind of would not mind that much if she did. If you know what I mean.

Maybelle swoops away and up onto the stage. "Maybelle, please stop," I whisper very soft. But she cannot hear me. Oh, well.

"Now, we are going to be announcing the parts for the play *The School-Yard Bully*," Mrs. Brice says. "Starting with the bully, which will be played by Antonio Fuerte." Everyone is turning and looking at Antonio.

"Hola!" he says.

And then Maybelle swoops right up onto that stage and switches off the microphone that Mrs. Brice is talking into!

"Now, for the rest of the parts," Mrs. Brice

is saying. But no one can hear her. On account of that microphone being shut right off.

"What?" I yell. "I cannot hear you!"

"Yeah!" yells Gordie Bloom. He is the meanest boy in room five. "You're Natalie's mom. You should have a great big huge mouth like her!" The substitute from room five has to take Gordie out of the auditorium. Because you are not really supposed to be saying things like that. Even if they are true. And even if everyone else might be thinking them in their heads.

But Mrs. Brice does not look upset. She just says, "Test, test, one, two, three, test," into the microphone. But we still cannot hear. She turns the microphone back on. Maybelle turns it back off. Then Maybelle flies away. When she comes back, she has a big pair of scissors! Scissors that are almost too big for her to hold! And then she cuts that microphone cord right in two!

"This microphone is broken," Mrs. Brice says.

"What?" Russ Robertson yells. "We cannot hear you!"

"I am the bully of this play!" Antonio yells. "And I will save you!"

He tries to get up. But I stop him. "Antonio," I say. "Bullies do not help, they only bully."

So Antonio sits back down.

"Did I do a good job, Hailey?" Maybelle asks. Now she is flying around my head.

I whisper, "Maybelle, you are very bad." But then I give her a secret high five.

- -

I thought that broken microphone was going

to save me. But it turns out that is not true. On account of that we just all go back to room five. So that Mrs. Brice can assign the parts in there.

In room five, all the children from room four have to sit on the carpet in the corner. The carpet is scratch, scratch, scratchy and not comfortable even one bit.

"Mr. Spaghetti," I say, "maybe we should go do this in room four."

"No," Mr. Spaghetti says. He is a good substitute, but only sometimes. Also, he is distracted by that broken microphone. No one can figure out how it got so broken. Yikes.

"Now," Mrs. Brice says. "As I was saying before something horrible happened to the microphone, Antonio Fuerte is playing the bully. Russ Robertson, Gordie Bloom, and Conner Bronston will be the kids who are being bullied on the school yard." I look over at Russ and he is very happy about this. Then Mrs. Brice says,

"Natalie Brice, Rachel Phillips, and Madison Papadakis will be the classroom children."

I am sitting very, very patient, waiting for her to say my name. But finally I cannot take it anymore. My hand goes shoot, shoot, shooting up into the air.

"What will Hailey Twitch have to be, please?" I give her a very charming look.

Mrs. Brice looks at me. She does not look too happy. Probably Natalie has told her lots of things about me. The same way that I have told my mom lots of things about Natalie. Probably she also remembers about something having to do with how Natalie Brice had to cancel her Ghost Hunting Party because of me. "Everyone else," she says, "will be in the chorus."

"The chorus?" I frown. "What is the chorus?"

"The chorus is the group of children who will sing the song when the bully comes onto the school yard," Mrs. Brice explains.

What?! Just one big group with everyone else in all the classes? That is not the way to stick out!

"Now, we will start rehearsal—"

But I am not done talking. I wave my hand back in the air. "Will the chorus get to wear sparkly pink dresses?" I ask.

"No," Mrs. Brice says.

"Do they get to carry magic wands?" I ask.

"No," she says.

"Do they get to have tiaras?"

"No, Hailey," she says. She is sounding a little bit grumpy. "They will not."

"Maybe," I say to Mrs. Brice, like I just thought of it. "Maybe we could do the play of *The Gingerbread Princess* instead! That play has all those things I just talked about."

"No," Mrs. Brice says. "*The School-Yard Bully* teaches us many lessons about life and friendship."

And that is the end of that.

Chapter Seven

Maybelle and the Out-of-Control Hose

When I get home from school, Maybelle is in the garage. She is working over on my dad's tool bench.

"Maybelle!" I say. "You are not allowed to be using my dad's tool bench!" What is wrong with that sprite? She already knows that! "My dad's tool bench is full of very dangerous and expensive things, young lady!"

"I know," Maybelle says. She is seeming very happy. "I am being fun and breaking rules."

Then I spot something that is sitting on that tool bench. Something very fluffy and white and spindly. "What is *that?*" I ask.

"That," Maybelle says, "is hair for Mr. Frisk!" She sounds very excited about that hair she made. She picks it up and flies around holding it. I try to grab it. But Maybelle will not let me.

"Stop that!" I say. "Come here and let me get a good look at it!"

"No!" Maybelle says. She is still flying. I am reach, reach, reaching, trying to snatch that hair right out of her hands.

"Maybelle Sinclair, if you do not let me get a good look at that hair, I will tell Mr. Tuttle that you are not fun at all!" I say.

Maybelle stops. Her mouth goes into the shape of an *o*. "That would not be nice," she says.

"Well, you are not being nice by not showing me the hair." I cross my arms and tap my foot. "You have a very hard decision to make, young lady," I tell her. Only Maybelle is not a young lady. She is a young sprite. Only she is not even a young sprite. She has been living in my magic castle for two hundred whole years. But "you have a very hard decision to make, young lady" is what my mom always says to me when I am in trouble. So I stick with it.

"Fine," Maybelle says. She drops the hair onto my head.

I reach up and pull it down. It is soft and white and just like real hair!

"Maybelle," I say. "You cannot give this to Mr. Frisk!"

"Why not?" Maybelle says. "It is part of the apology and of making a friend!"

"Yes, well, Mr. Frisk is bald, and I do not think he would like it too much if we gave him fake hair." I know all about bald heads. That is because my dad's friend Uncle Frank is bald and he is always complaining that he does not get any ladies to look at him because of it. He is very sensitive. He does not like kids asking him about his bald spot. Not at all, even. I learned this lesson the hard way.

"But I spent all day making that hair," Maybelle says. She is standing on the tool bench. "And besides," she says, "this wig is so gorgeous that Mr. Frisk will look absolutely lovely in it! And then he won't be able to resist being my friend, and I can get my magic back!" Maybelle looks very happy with herself.

"Sorry," I say, "but you cannot give that to him. We are already in too much trouble with Mr. Frisk. And I have to convince him by Monday to come and work on the play, and I do not know if that is even going to happen, so, sorry, but you are not giving him that hair!" I am standing my ground. I stamp my foot just for good measure.

Then my mom comes out to the garage.

"Hailey!" she says. "I did not know you were home. What are you doing out here?" Her eyes are moving over to my dad's tool bench.

"Oh, nothing," I say. I quick hide that fake hair behind my back.

"What are you hiding behind your back?" my mom wants to know. This is because she is very smart. She is remembering lots of times when I was hiding something bad behind my back.

"Oh, nothing," I say again. Maybelle flies down and snatches that hair right out of my hand.

"Hailey," my mom says. "Please show me what is behind your back."

I pull my hands out and show her that they are empty. "Here you go!" I say. "Empty hands for Hailey Twitch!" I turn them all around so she can see empty, empty, empty.

My mom frowns. Then she says, "Fine. Now please get inside and into your play clothes.

It is time for you to go and wash Mr. Frisk's driveway and then help him with his lawn."

- -

Getting dressed to go and help Mr. Frisk is not fun or funny. And that is because I have to wear clothes that I do not like. Those clothes are one pair of overalls with a hole in the knee. One black T-shirt that is for babies. And one pair of dirty old gray sneakers. I really do not like this outfit.

"That outfit is not fun or cute," Maybelle says when we are walking over to Edgar Frisk's.

"I know," I say. "But my mom made me."

Maybelle is wearing a pair of cute jeans and a pink T-shirt with her sparkly high heels. She stole them off Jessie Brody's doll. I do not know where or when, but Maybelle somehow got some style.

We march up

to Mr. Frisk's porch. I do not really like doing yard work. My dad is always making me help him rake leaves. Even though Kaitlyn is older and she should be doing that sort of stuff.

I ring the doorbell.

"Maybe he is not home," Maybelle says.

But Mr. Frisk opens that door right up.

"Hello," he says. He does not seem too friendly.

"Hello!" I say happily. "It's me, Hailey Twitch, here to help you." I do a twirl around to show off my work clothes.

"Here to fix your mess is more like it," Mr. Frisk grumbles.

Hmmm. I do not think this is going according to my plan to win him over.

"I think you and me got off on the wrong foot," I tell Mr. Frisk. Getting off on the wrong foot is when you accidentally make someone mad when you first meet them.

Even though you don't mean to, not even one little tiny bit.

"Go get the hose," Mr. Frisk says.

"Wow," Maybelle says. "He is not too friendly." She looks at Mr. Frisk. "But I would like him as a friend, because I really love his eyebrows."

"You do not pick friends because of how their eyebrows look!" I say.

"Who are you talking to?" Mr. Frisk says. Those big bushy eyebrows go into a frown. And then he reaches up and touches them.

"No one," I say real quick. "I was just going off to get the hose!" I decide to show Mr. Frisk that I am very fun and funny. Also that I would make a very good gingerbread princess. So I skip right over to the hose. Exactly the very same way a gingerbread princess would. Then I twirl the hose around and around and around.

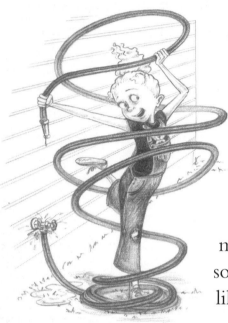

"Now come over here, Hailey," Mr. Frisk says.

"You can call me Hails for short," I tell him. This is because sometimes old people have a hard time remembering things like long names. Like my Grandpa Twitch who sometimes forgets things like my dad's birthday.

"Fine, fine," Mr. Frisk says. "Now bring it over here and start cleaning off all this chalk."

I walk very, very princess-like over to the driveway. I start twisting that hose and some water comes trick, trick, trickling out. I hold it over where the words spell out "I am sorry, Edgar Frisk!" It is going to be very sad to ruin all this hard work.

"That hose is stupid," Maybelle says. I want to tell her to please be quiet, but I don't. Because that is not what beautiful princesses do. "That water is not even coming out."

And then, before I can even stop her, Maybelle flies down and twists that hose right up! And water comes shooting out! And that water goes all over Mr. Frisk's face!

"Ahh!" Mr. Frisk shouts. "Ahhh! What are you DOING? HAILEY, STOP THAT, AHHHH!"

I finally get that water to stop. But when I turn to look, Mr. Frisk is a sop, sop, sopping wet mess. His white hair is very dripping. And his clothes are very dripping, too.

"I am so sorry, Mr. Frisk!" I say. "Would you please accept my apology?"

"No," Edgar Frisk says. He sounds like he is making a growl in his throat when he says that.

"No?" I ask. I am very confused. What is with this man? He definitely does not like apologies.

"No!" Mr. Frisk says. He is taking off his glasses. And he is trying to get the water off of them. "You have tried to serve me runny disgusting eggs. You have written all over my driveway. And now you have sprayed me with bitter cold water. What is *wrong* with you?"

"It was an accident," I say. "Cross my heart and promise." I do a cross over my heart so Mr.

Frisk knows it is true. "Maybe we should just move onto the yard work and come back to this later." And then I get distracted. This is because I am peek, peek, peeking into Edgar Frisk's garage. And right there, in one of his moving boxes, is a beautiful gold picture frame. And in that frame is a picture of a girl just my age!

"Hey!" I say. "Who is that, please? Is it one girl my very own same age?" I start to take one step toward that picture to get a better look.

But Mr. Frisk stops me. "Hailey," he says. "Please go home right now."

And so I do.

Chapter Eight

No More Ms. Nice Guy

Mr. Frisk does not even tell my mom what happened! That is a good thing because I do not get a punishment. But it is a bad thing because it means that Mr. Frisk thinks I am a lost cause. A lost cause is someone who you give right up on. It is someone who you do not want to help with the play *The Gingerbread Princess*.

The next day is Saturday. My mom wakes me up bright and early so we can go grocery shopping. I love to go grocery shopping! That is because I can pick out the things I want. Which means cereal. And chocolate milk. And maybe some good gummy bears.

But when we get to the store, my mom reminds me about something not so fun. And that is the new rule about healthy snacks.

"This milk is healthy," I tell her. "I heard all about it on a commercial." I put one big huge thing of chocolate milk right into the cart.

"No," my mom says. "White milk is healthy." She puts that chocolate milk back. And then she puts white milk into the cart.

"Does this mean no more pizza?" Maybelle asks. Maybelle loves pizza. It is her most very favorite food.

My mom takes me over to the fruit.

"Grapes are good, I guess," I say, very sad. I pick some up and put them in the cart. Then

Maybelle gets in the cart and starts eating them right off the tiny branches! That is not how you eat grapes. "Maybelle!" I say. "You better stop that."

It is a good thing my mom cannot hear. On account of that she is off looking at some carrots. And then I hear my mom say something horrible. And that is, "Well, hello, Patty, how nice to see you."

That is not the horrible part. Because I do not know anyone named Patty. The horrible part comes next. And that is when my mom says, "And, Natalie, aren't those interesting shoes!"

And then I turn to look. It turns out that Patty is Mrs. Brice! That is her grown-up name! And Natalie is with her, wearing her roller-skates shoes! Right in the store! Even though I am almost sure that is not allowed!

My mom is starting to talk to Mrs. Brice about boring grown-up things. Like what to make for dinner.

"Hello, Hailey," Natalie Brice says.

"Hello, Natalie," I say.

Maybelle is done eating grapes. And now she is sitting on the side of the cart. "I do not like Natalie," Maybelle says. "Also, I forgot to tell you that yesterday she stole your red marker right out of your desk and did not put it back."

I gasp. I was wondering where that red one went! I needed that marker to make a nose on

a clown I was drawing! Finally I had to make that nose green. And everyone knows that green is not a very good color for a nose.

"What are you doing here?" Natalie asks me.

"Oh, nothing," I say. "Just looking to buy some new markers. Especially *red ones*." I say it in a smart tone so that she gets the picture.

"We are shopping," Natalie says. "And then we are going to be picking out costumes for the school play."

I do not want to care about this. But I do. "What are those costumes going to look like?" I ask.

"Well, the schoolchildren like me are going to wear beautiful dresses," she says.

"That does not sound right," I say. "Schoolchildren should wear school clothes."

"Yeah," Maybelle says. She is back in the cart. And she is pulling a grape out of the bunch.

"It is my decision," Natalie says. "And so I decided on beautiful dresses."

I decide I will not ask her about what the chorus is going to wear. Because I have a feeling I do not want to know the answer to that question. But Natalie Brice tells me anyway.

"And the chorus is going to wear plain black heavy robes," she says. And then she twirls around on her roller-skate shoes!

I am trying to control myself. So that I do not get really mad. But I feel like maybe I am going to have a big tantrum. "Mom," I say. "I think we should be going now." I give my mom a look. A look that says it is time to get out of here before I lose it.

But before we can get out of there, something goes wrong. Maybelle picks up the grape she is holding and throws it right at Natalie's head!

"Owww," Natalie

says. "Owww, owww, owww, Hailey threw a grape at me!" She is yelling very loud. And holding her head. But for once, she cannot prove it. Because I am nowhere near those grapes.

"I think," my mom says, putting her hand on my back. "That we better go now."

- -

On the way home, I decide it is no more Ms. Nice Guy. Mostly this is because of those boring black robes I found out about.

So when I get home, I ask my mom for a special permission. And that permission is for Addie Jokobeck to come over. And my mom says yes! So I call Addie right up. And Addie says yes!

Then me and Maybelle go outside to wait for Addie.

"Do you have the rakes?" I ask Maybelle.

"Check," Maybelle says.

"Do you have all the big garbage bags?"

"Check," Maybelle says.

"Good," I say. "Now all we have to do is wait for Addie Jokobeck."

I have a new genius plan for when Addie Jokobeck gets over. And that is that we are going over to Mr. Frisk's house. We are going to pick apples from his apple trees and work on his garden without even being asked. This is to make up for the yard work I missed from yesterday! And Mr. Frisk will not be able to resist! I tried to warn him that I am not good at taking no for an answer. And now it is time to prove it.

I am bringing Addie Jokobeck because grown-ups really love her. They think she is a good influence. Addie Jokobeck does not know this plan yet. She thinks she is just coming over for a playdate. But she will say yes to it since I am the boss of her.

Me and Maybelle play a skip, skip, skipping game while we wait. Finally, after about three million years, Addie Jokobeck gets there. She is in her blue van with the shiny tires.

"Hi, Hailey," Mr. Jokobeck says. Mr. Jokobeck is very nice. He lets people have food fights. But me and him have had some rough patches. Like one time when I got Addie in trouble with Miss Stephanie. But it all worked out. And now it is behind us.

"Hi, Mr. Jokobeck," I say. I give him a big wave.

"Hi, Mr. Jokobeck!" Maybelle gives him a big wave, too.

"Addie, I will be back to pick you up in a couple hours," he says. He waves to my mom, who is coming out onto the porch.

Then he is gone.

"Now, girls," my mom says. "Do not leave this yard."

"Mom," I say. "Isn't it such a nice day out?" This is called distracting your parents. So that you can do what you want your own self.

"Yes," my mom says. Then she goes back inside. Right where she belongs.

"Are we going over to Edgar Frisk's? Are we going over to Edgar Frisk's?" Maybelle asks. She is getting very excited about all this.

"Hey, Addie," I say. "Do you see all those apple trees over there?" I point over to Mr. Frisk's house. If you look close, close, close you can see the tops of the trees sticking right up behind his fence.

"No," Addie says. She is looking at my house. "Let's go play dolls," she says.

"Um, well," I say. "Addie, do you want to know a secret?"

"Yes," Addie says. But she is looking just a little bit nervous. And that is because sometimes when I tell her secrets they do not turn out so well. But not this one! This plan is unable to fail!

"Remember how I told you about that one famous man who I am going to be getting to help with the play?"

"Yes," Addie says. She is still looking nervous in her face.

"Well, that guy's name is Edgar Frisk and he lives across the street," I say.

"Is he a voice on *Jim, the Dog Next Door?*" Addie asks.

"No," I say. I do not tell Addie that *Jim, the Dog Next Door* is a cartoon for babies. I will tell her that later maybe. When we are done weeding Mr. Frisk's lawn and picking his apples to get on his good side.

"Then how is he famous?" Addie asks.

"He is famous because he used to be in black-and-white movies. And also in some cake commercials. And I think he might love candy and sugar on account of that he has a big gumball machine right in his house."

"My mom loves old movies," Addie says. She nods. I knew Addie would understand about black-and-white movies! Those seem like they are right up her alley.

And then I decide to tell a tiny little fib. "He said he would help with the play if I helped him pick apples off of his trees and raked up his leaves." I cross my fingers behind my back so that the fib doesn't count. "You can help." I quick give her a smile.

"I don't know," Addie Jokobeck says. She looks over at those trees. "Aren't those apple trees very high?"

"Yes," I say. "But we will pick the ones

close to the ground." I give her an even big, big, bigger smile.

Addie thinks all about it. This is called weighing the pros and cons. "Okay," she finally says. "I will help you."

Yay! Addie really is a true friend! I take Addie's hand. And then we creep, creep, creep over to Mr. Frisk's house. Very soft like two little mice.

"Wait!" Addie yells when we are almost at the gate to Mr. Frisk's backyard. "Your mom said not to leave the yard!"

"She just forgot about how I was scheduled for some yard work," I tell her.

Addie is looking like maybe she does not believe this. Addie Jokobeck is very smart sometimes. "Also, it is a surprise to my mom, too," I tell her. "I am trying to be a good daughter."

"Oh." Addie still does not look that sure about all this. But I grab her hand and pull, pull, pull, pull her the rest of the way right over to Mr. Frisk's gate. That gate is not even locked! It swings right open, free as a bird! And so me and Addie walk in. And Maybelle, too.

We put our rakes down on the lawn. Because I have just spotted something better than a boring old rake. And that is a wheelbarrow!

"Addie, me and you will start picking the

apples and put them in here." I wheel that wheelbarrow right over and under one tree.

Addie looks up, up, up all the way to the sky almost. "I don't know, Hailey," she says. "Those trees go very high up."

"I think we can reach those apples if we jump." I look all around the backyard. "But it would be much better if me and you had a ladder."

"A ladder?!" Addie Jokobeck goes very pale in her face about that. Addie Jokobeck is very scared of things like ladders. She doesn't even hardly like sparkly glitter pencils.

"Just kidding," I say real quick. "We do not need a ladder. We can still get these apples."

I rush up and grab some apples from the bottom branches. And then I drop them into the wheelbarrow. Addie does it, too.

"See?" I say. "It is fun!"

"Hmm." Addie looks down at the apples.

"These apples are kind of small. I do not know if they are ready to be picked."

"Yes, they are ready," I say. "And if we do not pick them, Mr. Frisk will have to do it. All by himself, even. And he is very old and needs help." Then I add for good measure, "Mr. Frisk is so old he has bushy white eyebrows and no hair."

"Oh," Addie Jokobeck says. She nods. "I know all about that. Sometimes me and my mom go to the elderly home to sing to the old people."

"Yes, well, if we do not help Mr. Frisk pick these apples, he will have to go live there."

Addie's eyes get wide, wide, wide. And she starts picking apples. I do, too. And when Addie isn't looking, Maybelle swoops by the top of the tree. And she knocks a whole big bunch of apples down to the ground. *Plunk!* This makes me laugh, laugh, laugh.

"What was that?" Addie asks.

"Nothing," I say.

We pick, pick, pick those apples for a very long time.

Then the back door to Mr. Frisk's house opens. And Mr. Frisk is there!

"Oh, no!" I say. "Mr. Frisk, you are ruining the surprise!" I try to stand in front of that wheelbarrow so he does not see.

"WHAT HAVE YOU DONE?" Mr. Frisk screams. He runs off his back deck. He is holding his hands up on top of his bald head.

"We are helping you pick apples," I say. "Aren't they beautiful?" I look down in the

wheelbarrow. Uh-oh. There is one in there with a bite out of it. Mostly because hard work makes me hungry.

"We are doing all the work so that you do not have to go to the old folks home," Addie says. She holds an apple out to him. "Would you like me to mash this up for you like applesauce so that you can eat it?" Then she whispers to me, "Old people have no teeth."

"You have ruined my apple trees!" Mr. Frisk says. "The apples were not ready to be picked." He looks down at the ground. Right to where Maybelle dropped all those apples.

"Oh, those are fine," I say. I pick one up. It has

a dark spot on it. From where it hit the ground. "You can just cut that part out." I put it in the wheelbarrow and give him a very big smile.

"No," he says. "I cannot. Young lady, you… you…YOU HAVE REALLY CROSSED THE LINE THIS TIME."

And then the worst, worst, worst thing happens. And that is that I look up and see Maybelle flying over Mr. Frisk. And then Mr.

Frisk bends down in front of me to pick up some apples. And Maybelle flies down. And then she drops that wig she made for Mr. Frisk right on his head!

And when Mr. Frisk looks up, he thinks I did it!

Addie Jokobeck is busy picking up some apples, too. So she does not see Maybelle drop that wig on Mr. Frisk's head. And she does not see Mr. Frisk look up. And she does not see Mr. Frisk looking very, very, very mad at us.

"Addie," I say. I am taking one big step back. I grab her hand. And then I say, "RUN!"

Chapter Nine

Scrapes and Stings

Addie and I run. Right out of the backyard. Right through the open gate. Right across the street. Right toward my house. I am running very, very fast. And Addie Jokobeck is running fast, too. Almost faster than me. I did not know she had it in her.

Mr. Frisk is yelling behind us. He is saying, "Come back here! What is this you put on my head?" And then my feet are getting all tangled up and I am tripping and then all of a sudden I am falling on the ground. And my knee goes scrape, scrape, scraping across the road. It is burn, burn, burning, and when I look down there is a big scrape on my knee.

I do not do so well with bad scrapes.

"Come on, Hailey," Addie Jokobeck is saying. She is pulling on my arm. But I cannot stop looking at that blood. And then Mr. Frisk is behind me. He has caught right up to us!

"What is this?" he asks. He is holding that wig right up and shaking it. Then he notices the scrape.

And that is when I start to cry. Because that knee hurts very, very bad. I am not a baby. But sometimes a girl cannot help it. Especially if there is blood involved. Even just a teeny-tiny bit.

"Owww!" I wail.

Mr. Frisk crouches down next to me and takes a good look at it. "That little thing?" he asks. "It'll be just fine."

"Oh, Hailey," Addie Jokobeck says. "Your poor knee." She is petting my hair like a good friend.

"Poor knee?" Mr. Frisk says. "It's just a little scrape. Nothing to cry about."

But I am crying now. And a big tear drops onto my knee.

"Oh, no, oh, no, oh, no," Maybelle says. I don't know if she's ever seen anyone get hurt before.

"You need to get inside," Mr. Frisk says. "And put a Band-Aid on it. Come on, I'll help you home." He holds his hand out.

"Nooooo." I sniffle. "My mom will be very mad. And then she will put peroxide on my knee, and IT WILL BURN." Peroxide is a very burny thing that moms are always loving to put on scrapes. And it will hurt, hurt, hurt. Also, she will be mad about me picking all those apples.

"Did you know," Addie Jokobeck asks, "that one slice of apple pie has eighteen grams of sugar? Doesn't that sound so delicious and tasty? You could make some pie with the apples we picked!" That's when I figure out that Addie is trying to distract Mr. Frisk with thoughts of sugar! She remembers what I told her about how he likes it! She is a very good and smart friend, that Addie Jokobeck.

Mr. Frisk sighs. He is wearing a pair of very big black shoes. I can see them very up close because I am on the ground.

"Come on," he says. "Come and sit on my porch for a minute." He helps me up. And I limp, limp, limp over to his porch. Me and

Addie Jokobeck sit down on the bench Mr. Frisk has out there.

Then Mr. Frisk goes inside.

"Do you think he's going to tell our parents?" Addie asks. She is looking very nervous.

"What do you think?" I say. Because the answer to that question is, of course, yes.

"Just be polite," Maybelle says. "And try not to get too upset. You need to hold it together." Easy for her to say. She is not the one that has a scraped-up knee. Plus, Mr. Frisk can't even see or hear her. She has it very easy, that Maybelle Sinclair.

When Mr. Frisk comes back out, he is not holding that wig anymore. He is holding a box of Band-Aids. And a tube of something. And then I get it. Mr. Frisk is going to put whatever is in that tube right on my leg!

"No, thank you," I say, starting to stand up. "I do not need any of that tube, thank you very much." But my knee hurts too much. I plop back down with an "Ow!"

"One brownie has 170 whole calories," Addie says to Mr. Frisk. She gives him a big grin.

"Is that so?" Mr. Frisk asks.

Addie nods. "And a piece of rock candy is pretty much pure sugar."

"Thank you, Addie," I say. "That is very helpful. All those candies sound just delicious and we should maybe leave Mr. Frisk to go and eat some of them. And so now we will be leaving..."

"Hailey," Mr. Frisk says. He holds up the scary tube. "This will not sting you. Now don't be a baby."

"This will not sting you" and "don't be a baby" are what grown-ups say right before they do something that is going to sting you.

"That is quite all right," I say. "I do not need any of that tube since my knee is fine." I turn to Addie. "Addie, please get right up and come over here and help me home." Addie gets right up.

My knee isn't hurting as bad as it was at first. But on the other hand it is hard to walk home with a scrape when you know your mom might be there waiting to be very mad at you and maybe even use some peroxide to get her revenge.

"Hailey," Mr. Frisk says. "This will not sting you, I promise."

"Addie," I say quietly. "I would like you to hold my hand, please."

So Addie puts her hand out. And I squeeze it very, very hard. And Mr. Frisk puts that cream on my knee! And he is right! It does not even hurt one bit! Then he puts the Band-Aid on. It is just a plain boring brown Band-Aid. One that does not have butterflies on it. Or princesses. Or party hats. But that is okay. I will change it later.

"Thank you, Mr. Frisk," I say. "I feel better already." It is true. I wipe my nose on my sleeve. And then I start to feel bad. Very, very bad. Mr. Frisk is being very nice to me. And I have done nothing but make trouble for him. And so then I start to sniffle again.

"What is it, Hailey?" Addie Jokobeck asks. "Why are you crying? Is it your knee still?"

"No," I say. "I am crying because Mr. Frisk is being so nice to me," I say. "And I was...I was...I ruined your apples and your driveway and I tried to make you eat some very disgusting raw eggs!" Addie Jokobeck looks shocked by all this. "And also now you are going to tell my mom and now I am going to be in very big trouble, young lady, and then me and Addie will not be able to be friends on account of I'm a bad influence."

"And me, too! I will be in trouble with Mr. Tuttle!" Maybelle says. But, of course, that is really the least of my problems right now.

"Okay, okay," Mr. Frisk says. "Geez, I never saw such a bunch of worrywarts." He frowns his big bushy eyebrows. "Hailey, I will not tell your mom about this."

"You won't?" I jump up and down. Suddenly my knee is feeling much better.

"I will not," Mr. Frisk says. "As long as you promise this time to stay out of my yard. And I mean it. If you do not, I will tell your mom all about what you did today. And about what happened yesterday."

"I promise," I say.

"I promise," Addie Jokobeck says.

"I think I am going to have to find a new friend," Maybelle says.

Then I pull a piece of candy out of my pocket. "Here," I say to Mr. Frisk. "I brought this for you."

But Mr. Frisk just frowns. He is suddenly very grumpy again. "No, thank you," he says. "I…" But he doesn't say anything more than that. That is called not using your words. And then he goes inside and shuts the door.

Chapter Ten

- -

True Friends

I am so excited about Mr. Frisk not telling my mom that I forget all about the very biggest problem. And that problem is that Mrs. Brice is still going to be the boss of the play. But when it is time for school on Monday, I remember it right away. And I am so grumpy that I am stomp, stomp, stomping all around the house.

"Hailey," Maybelle says. "You should not be doing all that stomping around like that. Your mom or your dad or Kaitlyn will hear you."

"Hailey!" Kaitlyn yells from her room right

next door. "Stop all that stomping around!" She is so annoyed that she does not even call me Hails.

"Told you so," Maybelle says.

"One—you are not the boss of me, Maybelle!" I say, wagging a finger. "Two—you are going to be in very big trouble when I tell Mr. Tuttle that you have not even made one friend!"

Ding-dong. The doorbell rings.

"I wonder who *that* is," I say. It is very much too early for guests.

Maybelle and I run to the window. To see who is at the door. And when we look down we see one very bald head. A bald head that belongs to Edgar Frisk!

"Uh-oh," I say. Then I run, run, run down the stairs to get to the door before my mom. I hope Mr. Frisk has not changed his mind about our plan for him not to be a tattletale.

"Oh, hello, Mr. Frisk," I say in my most calm voice.

"Hello, Hailey," he says. "I wanted you to know that the apples you picked yesterday were fine after all." He is holding a big apple pie. He holds it right out to me. "So I baked this pie last night. I thought your family would like to have it."

"Oh, thank you," I say. I take that pie and then set it down real quick on the table that is by the door. "Okay, well, bye!"

I start to push that door closed. But it is too late. Because my mom has spotted Mr. Frisk! And also she has heard the big commotion at the door.

"Hailey," she says, "do not be rude. Invite Mr. Frisk in."

"Oh, he has to go," I say. "He cannot stay long. He is late for something very important."

"Hailey," Mr. Frisk whispers. "Don't worry. I am not going to tell her."

"Oh, phew," I say. Now I can relax. And maybe even have a breakfast slice of that delicious pie.

"How nice of you to bring us a pie," my mom says. "Would you like to stay and have a slice?"

"No, thank you," Mr. Frisk says. "I'm actually not supposed to be eating sugar anymore." He looks very sad about this.

"That's why you didn't want that piece of candy I tried to give you!" I say.

"Yes," he says.

"But what about that big gumball machine you have?" I ask.

"Sugar-free gumballs," he says, sighing. "They're not the same."

"I understand," I say and give his hand a good pat. "It's like when I wish I was wearing Natalie Brice's roller-skate shoes because I don't have a pair my own self."

"It is not too late, it is not too late!" Maybelle says. "You can ask him to come to school today and be my friend!"

"Excuse me, Mr. Frisk," I say. "But what are you doing this morning?"

"Why...nothing," Mr. Frisk says.

"Well," I say. "As you might remember, we are having a class play." And then I decide it is time to tell the truth, the whole truth, and nothing but the truth. "That is the main reason that I have been trying so hard to make friends." I look at my mom and then decide to just go for it. "I know you are a famous actor, and I was thinking maybe you could come to my school and help us do our play." I quick cross my fingers behind my back.

"No, Hailey," my mom says. "Mr. Frisk is very busy. And I am sure he does not have time to come to your school this morning."

"Yes, but if he does not then we are going to have to do the play of *The School-Yard Bully*!" This is my last chance. "And some people will have to wear big black robes and that is not very fun or funny. Not like *The Gingerbread Princess,* which is really the most perfect play when you think about it."

"*The Gingerbread Princess?*" Mr. Frisk asks.

"Yes," I say. "That is the play we were supposed to do, until Mrs. Brice and Mr.

Spaghetti changed the whole plan! It is about a very beautiful princess who meets some gingerbread men and then she—"

"I know what it's about," Mr. Frisk says.

"You shouldn't interrupt," I tell him. "That is one of the manners that we learned in first grade."

"Hailey!" my mom says.

"Sorry," I say.

But Edgar Frisk just laughs. I have never seen him laugh before! It is a very deep laugh, and his whole eyebrows are moving up and down. "You are right, Hailey," he says. "I shouldn't interrupt. I just got excited because my granddaughter once played the part of the gingerbread princess."

"She did?!" He must be talking about one girl who is just about my own age! "Is that the girl in the picture I saw in your garage when I was peeking in there?"

"Hailey!" my mom says. "You were spying into Mr. Frisk's garage?"

"No, she wasn't," Mr. Frisk says. Then he winks at me. "And you know what? I think I have some time this morning, after all."

I grin. And then Maybelle gives me a high five behind my back.

— — — — — — — — — — — — — — — — — — — —

Mr. Frisk is coming to my school! Now everyone will know that I did not tell a lie. Everyone including Antonio Fuerte and Russ Robertson and Addie Jokobeck and Natalie Brice. I am so excited that I am skip, skip, skipping into the school yard.

Mr. Frisk is going to come and meet us later. And so I am bragging as soon as I get out near the swing set. I am pretty much bragging to anyone that will listen.

"Did you know that a famous actor named

Edgar Frisk is coming to our school to be in charge of the play?" I ask.

"Is he going to let me still be the bully?" Antonio asks. His black eyes are looking very nervous.

"I do not know," I say. "You will have to just ask him." I decide I will let Mr. Frisk break that bad news, thank you very much.

"Hailey Twitch, that is a big lie," Natalie Brice says. She is wearing her shoes with the roller skates on them.

"You are not allowed to wear those shoes in the classroom, Natalie," I tell her. "So you better take them off before you go inside." I feel like maybe I am going to have a tantrum. But I am able to control it. Since Mr. Frisk is going to be coming here soon. And since we will be doing the play *The Gingerbread Princess,* which is much better than a play with bullies.

"That is a lie about that famous man,"

Natalie says again. Even though I already heard her the first time. Also, she is ignoring the part I told her about how she is breaking the rules.

"Well, you will just have to see," I tell her.

But Mr. Frisk does not come all during the

Pledge of Allegiance. He does not come during any of our morning spelling. Or math. Or science. And when it is time to go to the auditorium to work on the play, Edgar Frisk is still not there!

"See," Natalie Brice says. "I told you that he was not coming." She goes march, march, marching by me. She is wearing very pretty gray shoes that look like ballet shoes. Her roller-skate shoes are in her cubby. Mr. Spaghetti made her put them away. But honestly that did not even make me feel better one little bit.

"It is okay, Hailey," Addie Jokobeck says. She squeezes my hand. "It will be fun to be in the chorus."

I want to scream, scream, scream and have a good tantrum. Because it's looking like Mr. Frisk told a lie! He is not coming! I want to maybe take that pie and give it back to him. Because not showing up is not what true friends do!

"Does that mean me and Mr. Frisk are not

friends anymore?" Maybelle asks. She is looking very nervous.

"Yes," I say. "It does. Because friends do not do that to other friends."

Wait a minute! I am walking down the aisle in the auditorium. And I see Mr. Spaghetti! He is standing up on the stage! And standing right next to him is Edgar Frisk! And Mr. Frisk is holding a very important clipboard! Also, he is wearing a hat! A fancy hat that looks very warm and covers up his bald head. That hat is probably a better choice than that cotton-ball wig that Maybelle made him.

"Mr. Frisk!" I yell. "Over here, Mr. Frisk! It is me, Hailey Twitch!"

"Hailey," Mr. Spaghetti says. "Please, we are using indoor voices."

"Mr. Frisk," I whisper. "Over here!"

Mr. Frisk waves. All the children sit down in their seats.

And then Mrs. Brice walks out on the stage with those two! It is Mr. Spaghetti and Mrs. Brice and Edgar Frisk! All up onstage together!

"Oh, my goodness," Mrs. Brice gasps when she sees Mr. Frisk. "You're Edgar Frisk!" She grabs his hand and shakes, shakes, shakes it up and down. "I am your biggest fan. What are you doing here?"

"I came to help out with the play," Mr. Frisk says. "I am friends with Hailey Twitch."

"Wow," Mrs. Brice says. "I am so honored to be working with you."

And then comes the very best part. "I was

thinking," Mr. Frisk says, "that we could maybe do the play of *The Gingerbread Princess*. Have you read it? There are many more parts to give out. That way more children could be involved."

"Yes, yes, of course. Whatever you think is right," Mrs. Brice says.

Natalie Brice is hearing all of this. And she is looking very mad, mad, mad.

"I think," Maybelle says, "that me and you are friends with Mr. Frisk now."

"I think," I whisper back, "that you are right."

"Now," Mr. Frisk says. He looks down at his big clipboard. "We will think about who is going to play what part."

I sit very still and cross my fingers hard. But when it is time to give out the parts, it turns out that Addie Jokobeck will play the part of the gingerbread princess. At first, I am very, very upset. But then I look over. And Addie Jokobeck has two small red spots on her cheeks.

Which is what Addie gets when she is secretly very happy. Like this one time when I gave her my very best sparkly pencil.

So I reach over and squeeze her hand. It turns out that I get the part of one of the gingerbread children! Which is fine with me! I am going to be very good at that part.

And then we are all lining up and getting ready to go up on the stage for the first time!

"Hey, Mr. Frisk," I say to him when I get up there. "I like your hat."

"Yes, well," Mr. Frisk says. He pats his head. "I needed something a little more, uh, *sturdy* than the wig you gave me." And then he gives me a wink.

Maybelle is smiling real big. "That wig was my idea!" she whispers at me, flapping all around. "I am definitely friends with Mr. Frisk. Right, Hailey?"

"Yes," I say. "You definitely are."

Then I go clomping up the stairs to the stage.

"Now," Mr. Frisk says. "First we will figure out the lines."

"Can the gingerbread children wear sparkly pink buttons on their gingerbread costumes?" I ask.

Mrs. Brice starts to scratch her chin. But Mr. Frisk says, "Of course!"

Then Addie Jokobeck gets up and practices

some lines. She is very good at being the gingerbread princess, I must admit.

And when it comes time for me to do my one line, I get to say in a very worried voice, "But the evil witch will come with her pet wolf and eat your house!"

I am very good at delivering that line if I do say so myself.

We rehearse for one whole hour! And it is very fun! And I can tell Mr. Frisk thinks I am the very best one of the gingerbread children!

And Antonio Fuerte is not even upset at not getting to be the school-yard bully. Because he gets to play the part of the evil witch's husband.

Even Natalie Brice is happy, because she gets to play the evil witch, and she is very good at it.

- -

When rehearsal is over, it is time to take the

bus home. I sit in the very last seat. I am still thinking all about my gingerbread costume. I am going to decorate it with pink glitter candy buttons. I am so distracted thinking about those beautiful sparkly gorgeous buttons that at first, I do not even notice that Mr. Tuttle is there.

"Good afternoon, Hailey," he says.

"Mr. Tuttle!" I whisper. "You have to go away! You cannot be popping up on the bus! A lot of kids are going to be coming onto this bus very soon!"

"Yes, well, this cannot wait." Mr. Tuttle looks down at his clipboard. He looks very scary. "Maybelle," he says. "Is it true that you have made a friend called Edgar Frisk?"

"Why don't you ask me?" I say. "I am the one that is the boss of Maybelle about this."

"Okay," Mr. Tuttle agrees. "Did Maybelle make a friend?"

"Yes," I say. "Maybelle did make a friend." Mr. Tuttle looks at me. "She won him over with a wig," I explain.

"Right." Mr. Tuttle writes something down on his paper. "Well, Maybelle," he says. "You will now be allowed to have your magic for two weeks. And we will see how it goes."

"Two weeks!" Maybelle says. "But I thought I was getting my magic back forever!"

"Don't argue, young lady," I say. "Or you will not get your magic back at all."

"Hailey is right," Mr. Tuttle says. "Two weeks. And then I will be back to let you know how it went." And then he poofs right away!

"Maybelle!" I say. "You got your magic back! Quick, give me some shoes with roller skates on the bottom!"

But then Russ Robertson comes bouncing all the way to the back of the bus! Before Maybelle can even do anything.

"Hi, Hailey," he says. "Can I sit with you?"

"Well, Russ," I say. "Today really is not a good day for me if you know what I mean."

"Hahaha," Russ says. He plops right down next to me.

Maybelle is now holding a wand! Maybelle somehow got a magic wand! I want to ask her where she got that wand. But I cannot while Russ is right there.

And then I look down. I am hoping to see roller-skate shoes. But I do not. All I see are my regular shoes. With my regular socks. Only now one sock is white, like it was when I put it on

152

this morning. And one sock is blue, NOT like when I put it on this morning.

Maybelle is looking at her wand. "I don't understand what happened," she says. "I was trying to give you roller-skate shoes."

Uh-oh. I think Maybelle having her magic back might not be so fun after all...

Acknowledgments

Thank you so, so much to:

My agent, Alyssa Eisner Henkin, for being the best agent a girl could ask for.

My editor, Daniel Ehrenhaft, for pushing me to make Hailey's adventures the best they can be.

The whole Sourcebooks team, including Dominique Raccah, Kelly Barrales-Saylor, Kristin Zelazko, Kay Mitchell, and Carrie Gellin, for all their hard work.

Suzanne Beaky, for the amazing illustrations.

My sisters Krissi and Kelsey, for being my best friends.

My mom, for always being there.

And Mandy Hubbard, Jessica Burkhart, Erin Dionne, Kevin Cregg, and Scott Neumyer for their support.

Be sure to read Hailey's
first adventure!

978-1-4022-2444-7 • $6.99 U.S. • $8.99 CAN • £3.99 UK

About the Author

Lauren Barnholdt loves reading, writing, and anything pink and sparkly. She's never had a magic sprite, but she *does* have four guinea pigs. She lives outside Boston with her husband. Visit her website and say hello at www.laurenbarnholdt.com.

About the Illustrator

Suzanne Beaky grew up in Gahanna, Ohio, and studied illustration at Columbus College of Art and Design. Her expressive illustrations are commissioned by children's book, magazine, and educational publishers worldwide. She and her husband live in Kirksville, Missouri, with their cats who insist on sitting in her lap while she works and often step in her paint.